Dream-of-Jade
THE EMPEROR'S CAT

Lloyd Alexander

Illustrated by D. Brent Burkett

Cricket Books
Chicago

For my dear cats who told me these tales
—L.A.

Text copyright © 2005 by Lloyd Alexander
Illustrations copyright © 2005 by D. Brent Burkett
All rights reserved
Printed and bound in Singapore
Designed by Ron McCutchan
Fouth printing, 2012

Library of Congress Cataloging-in-Publication Data
Alexander, Lloyd.
    Dream-of-Jade : the Emperor's cat / by Lloyd Alexander; illustrated by D. Brent Burkett.—1st ed.
        p. cm.
    "Sections of this book were first published in the October, November, and December 1976 issues (volume 4, numbers 2–4) of *Cricket* magazine."

    Summary: Follows the adventures of a Chinese cat who became the emperor's good friend and advisor.
    ISBN 0-8126-2736-9 (hardcover)
[1. Cats—Fiction. 2. Kings, queens, rulers, etc.—Fiction. 3. China—History—Fiction.] I. Burkett, D. Brent, ill. II. Title.
    PZ7.A3774Dt 2005
    [Fic]—dc22
                                    2004024068

How Dream-of-Jade Looked at the Emperor

IN THE FORBIDDEN City of the Celestial Emperor Kwan-Yu lived a white cat with such beautiful green eyes that she was called Dream-of-Jade. Slender, graceful, with a charming smile and melodious purr, she came and went unhindered throughout the palace, pavilions, gardens, and orchards—wherever she pleased—save the Imperial Chambers and Throne Room. She had never seen the Emperor, for only councilors and officials of highest rank were permitted in the Celestial Presence.

Kwan-Yu, no doubt, is a grand personage, thought Dream-of-Jade. Lord of the Middle Kingdom, Embodiment of Nine Heavenly Virtues, Tranquil Carp in the Pool of Crystal Wisdom, and so on. But how difficult to admire an Emperor for the most part invisible.

As curious as she was beautiful, and as determined as she was curious, Dream-of-Jade resolved to see the Emperor for herself. Quick and light on her paws, she slipped easily past the men-at-arms guarding the portals of the Throne Room and made her way inside. Finding it empty, she set about exploring the galleries, balconies, and alcoves. She padded over the flagstones and observed that while the floor had been scrubbed until it gleamed, the tiled ceiling was in serious disrepair.

Dream-of-Jade continued her inspection, climbing atop the bronze dragons crouching beside Kwan-Yu's throne of gold, ebony, and ivory until, at last, she jumped onto the great throne itself.

"Poor fellow," said Dream-of-Jade. "What a draft from the ceiling! How uncomfortable Kwan-Yu must be if he is obliged to sit here any length of time."

A moment later the huge doors of carved teakwood were flung open. Amid the crashing of gongs and trillings of flutes, the Celestial Kwan-Yu and his retainers entered the hall in solemn procession. Dream-of-Jade made no attempt to hide. From her seat on the throne she could not have had a better view, so there she remained.

The Embodiment of Nine Heavenly Virtues, she saw, appeared scarcely of a size to contain them all, for Kwan-Yu was slight of stature and, clearly, under his silken skull-cap he was bald as a lemon. He walked stiffly, burdened by a gown heavy with gold embroidery and crusted with gems.

His followers were no less gorgeously attired in brocaded robes and bright sashes. Nevertheless, these haughty mandarins walked with heads bowed and eyes fixed on the ground, never venturing an upward glance—it being long custom that no one, even of the most exalted station, dare gaze directly upon the face of a Celestial Emperor.

Dream-of-Jade well knew of this custom. However, she considered it altogether foolish and, in her case, especially so, since she had come for the express purpose of seeing Kwan-Yu. Therefore, instead of lowering her eyes, she continued to look squarely and steadily at the Emperor.

Kwan-Yu, for his part, had been withdrawn into his own thoughts. Not until he drew closer to his throne did he notice Dream-of-Jade. He then halted abruptly, frowned, drew his hands from the sleeves of his gown, and clapped thrice to summon his Chief Minister.

"Most Honorable Yin-Chuan," said the Emperor, "there would appear to be a cat sitting on my throne. Moreover, it would seem this cat is looking at me."

Bowing deeply, at great pains to keep his eyes from the Emperor, the Chief Minister peered at Dream-of-Jade, puffed out his cheeks, then cautiously replied, "Son of Heaven, your observation is highly illuminating. There does, in fact, appear to be a feline creature so situated and performing the ocular activity you have so graciously called to my unworthy attention. Allow me to withdraw and prepare a full report on this extremely disturbing event."

"Yin-Chuan," declared the Emperor, while Dream-of-Jade continued undisturbed to study him, "I desire this matter corrected without delay."

"Celestial Highness," answered the Chief Minister, "my investigation will begin immediately, and my preliminary findings will be made within three weeks after the third quarter of the moon."

"What are you telling me?" retorted the Emperor. "That I must wait until autumn before I can sit on my throne? And be stared at in the meanwhile by this cat?"

At this, Dream-of-Jade rose gracefully to her feet and bowed most charmingly to Kwan-Yu. "Celestial Highness," she said, "one could, no doubt, pass many days in contemplation of Your Radiant Countenance."

"Many days?" replied Kwan-Yu, not at all displeased by Dream-of-Jade's answer. "Ah—yes, very likely to gain the full effect would require a certain amount of time."

"Highness," put in the Chief Minister, glaring at Dream-of-Jade, "need I remind you the presence of this feline is strictly forbidden? In addition, this audacious animal has compounded one unpardonable offense with yet another—namely, looking at you."

"Alas," Dream-of-Jade sighed, "I know the offenses are very grave. Nevertheless, the opportunity to observe the magnificent Embodiment of all Nine Heavenly Virtues was irresistible."

"Yes, there you have the explanation," said Kwan-Yu to the Chief Minister. "As there is no harm done, we shall forgive this highly intelligent and perceptive cat and grant her our Celestial Permission to depart."

"Quite impossible, Your Highness," declared Yin-Chuan. "The matter has gone too far. The case must be adjudicated according to regulation and protocol. There is, of course, no question regarding the essential jurisprudence. The punishment is predetermined: immediate execution. Once that small detail is concluded, we shall have ample time to consider the case in the calm wisdom of retrospect."

Kwan-Yu, meanwhile, was finding himself with an overwhelming desire to stroke the silky fur of Dream-of-Jade. At the words of Yin-Chuan, however, he drew back his hand and turned to the Chief Minister. "Execution? This delightful creature? The penalty seems to me rather excessive, when her only fault was a perfectly understandable inability to resist gazing upon her Emperor."

"Without questioning the judgment of the Honorable Yin-Chuan," put in Dream-of-Jade, "allow me to suggest that my crime may be outweighed by the merit gained in saving the Emperor's life."

"This cat speaks nonsense," declared Yin-Chuan. "Save the Emperor's life? From what? Your Highness is guarded, protected, sustained in every way. No ill can possibly befall you."

"Lord of the Middle Kingdom," said Dream-of-Jade, "how fortunate your mandarins keep their eyes firmly on the ground. Thus they will be spared the unhappy prospect of observing the serious, and very likely fatal, damage to Your Celestial Person. Directly above Your Celestial Head, the tiles of the Imperial Ceiling are loose and may fall at any moment."

"Ridiculous! Impossible!" sputtered Yin-Chuan. "A miserable cat dares to insult the Imperial Ceiling—and, by extension, Your Imperial Self!"

"As it is written in the *Chronicles of Perfumed Zephyrs*," said Kwan-Yu, "a small insult is preferable to a broken head. Look into the matter immediately."

9

"As you command," answered Yin-Chuan. "I shall summon the Imperial Architect, the Imperial Surveyor, and the Imperial Geometrician. We shall give the question our undivided attention, and Your Highness will receive a memorandum of our transactions within six months."

During this exchange, Dream-of-Jade's sharp ears detected a faint crackling and grating sound from overhead. Instantly, she sprang from the throne into the arms of the astonished Emperor, who stumbled backward and nearly found himself in a heap on the Imperial Floor.

At the same moment, the loose tiles that Dream-of-Jade had observed when first she entered the Throne Room gave way and plummeted from the ceiling. The heavy fragments went crashing down upon the throne exactly as Dream-of-Jade had warned.

Tranquil Carp though he was, Kwan-Yu started in alarm, but he was wise enough to see how narrowly he had escaped with a whole skin. Still keeping Dream-of-Jade in his arms, he turned angrily to his terrified mandarins, who kowtowed and struck their heads against the flagstones.

"This cat has served me better today than any of you," declared the Emperor. "I hereby grant to her and all her descendants the unique privilege of looking upon me and all my descendants whenever and as often as they desire."

"Celestial Highness," replied Dream-of-Jade, "your favor honors me and, should I ever have descendants, I am sure they will be every bit as impressed as I am. But I suggest that all your subjects be granted the same privilege."

"Out of the question!" cried the Chief Minister. "Since the Reign of the First Emperor, no one has been permitted to look upon the illustrious features of a Celestial Monarch. Should this be allowed, who knows what will come of it?"

"Honorable Yin-Chuan," replied Dream-of-Jade, "if you and your colleagues had not been constrained to go about with your noses to the ground, you might better have looked around you and seen as clearly as I did."

"It will be as this cat desires," said the Emperor, smiling down at Dream-of-Jade. "What she suggests is not without merit, and I recognize a certain usefulness in it. But, Honorable Cat, tell me this: Might not my subjects find the sight of their Divine Ruler too overwhelming?"

"Highness," Dream-of-Jade replied, "I am quite sure they will grow used to it."

The Emperor then bestowed on Dream-of-Jade the rank of Imperial Cat. From that day on, he kept her always with him. When he held court, she curled on his lap; she shared his meals at the Imperial Table and slept at the foot of the Imperial Couch. The mandarins and ministers, even Yin-Chuan, were required to give her the same respect they gave to the Emperor. Dream-of-Jade accepted all these honors with grace and modesty, though sometimes she wondered what would have become of her if the tiles had not been loose.

How Dream-of-Jade
Cured the Emperor

THE EMPEROR KWAN-YU was in low spirits. Sleepless, without appetite, he held his aching Celestial Head and moaned over the state of his Celestial Liver. Dream-of-Jade, his beloved white cat, soon understood the nature of the ailment and the best remedy for it.

"Son of Heaven," she said, "allow me to prescribe a treatment that will restore Your Honorable Well-Being."

But Chief Minister Yin-Chuan overheard this, and his jowls trembled indignantly as he said to the cat, "A cat cure an emperor? Imperial Feline, confine yourself to the practice of mouse catching, not medicine. His Highness must be treated only by the most esteemed physicians."

So, at the insistence of the Chief Minister, who then left on urgent state business, the most illustrious practitioners were summoned to the Imperial Chambers.

12

First came the Venerable Doctor Pang-Fou, carrying scrolls and charts and calculating beads. Pang-Fou kowtowed to the Emperor; then, without a further glance at his patient, he began spreading his charts over the floor.

"Honorable Pang-Fou," Dream-of-Jade courteously asked, "why do you not examine His Celestial Highness or even take his pulse?"

"There is no need for such earthly trifles," intoned Pang-Fou. "I have cast the Imperial Horoscope, and by every cosmological sign, His Highness may look forward to a glorious recovery of strength and health."

"That is excellent news," Dream-of-Jade replied. "But, Venerable Pang-Fou, how soon may the Emperor expect this happy occurrence?"

"Allowing for the intercalation of equinox and solstice," Pang-Fou declared, "when the Year of the Hare enters the House of the Dragon—in precisely four hundred and twenty-five years and seventeen days."

Hearing this, Kwan-Yu groaned wretchedly, but Dream-of-Jade bowed politely and said to Pang-Fou, "We are grateful, Farseeing Astrologer, for the benefit of your astral wisdom. You may take your leave of us."

Pang-Fou hesitated, frowning. "Honorable Cat, there still remains the matter of my fee. This horoscope foretells I am to be generously rewarded."

"So you shall be," said Dream-of-Jade, "in the same measure as the value of your services."

"And when," asked Pang-Fou, "may I expect this munificent payment?"

"Consult your own horoscope," said Dream-of-Jade, "and you will see, with absolute confidence, that you will be paid in precisely four hundred and twenty-five years— and seventeen days."

Dream-of-Jade then dismissed the Venerable Pang-Fou, as much out of sorts as he was out of pocket. Before she could again urge the Emperor to hear her own suggestion, there arrived the Illustrious Doctor Fo, who strode briskly into the chamber.

Unlike the astrologer, Doctor Fo not only took the Celestial Pulse, he pinched and prodded, thumped and tapped so vigorously that Kwan-Yu protested he felt worse than before.

"Your condition is very grave, Son of Heaven," said Doctor Fo. "But, mercifully, I have with me certain rare and marvelous potions to bring about an unfailing cure.

Here is powdered unicorn horn, to be taken thrice daily. And here, extract of hippogriff and ointment of phoenix. These medications are priceless."

"As one might expect," said Dream-of-Jade. "However, for the Emperor's health there can be no counting of cost."

"How well you understand the requirements of our profession," said Doctor Fo. "Now, as for my reimbursement . . ."

"The amount of your reimbursement is exceeded only by our gratitude," said Dream-of-Jade. "The Emperor will gladly sign an order to the Imperial Treasury, bestowing upon you the sum of one hundred thousand pieces of pure chiang-liang."

"Chiang-liang?" cried the Illustrious Fo. "There is no such substance. It does not exist!"

"It is as rare, marvelous, and priceless as your own medicines," Dream-of-Jade returned, "and it exists just as surely as the creatures that have provided your ingredients."

While servants escorted the sputtering and furious Doctor Fo from the chamber, the Learned Doctor Ming-Tao was announced. So feeble he was—tottering on spindly legs, coughing and snuffling pitifully—that Dream-of-Jade considered Ming-Tao would be well advised to consult a physician himself.

"The Emperor's condition is desperate," wheezed Ming-Tao. "Nevertheless, take heart. I know the cure. The Emperor must henceforth subsist exclusively on lichee nuts. For breakfast: lichee nuts. At noon: lichee nuts. For dinner: lichee nuts."

"That seems a rather limited diet," said Dream-of-Jade. "Are you certain of its benefits?"

"I follow the diet myself," replied Ming-Tao. "Let the Emperor profit by my example."

"Thank you for your advice," said Dream-of-Jade. "You may leave us now. But you will be rewarded with many tokens of our gratitude: a lifetime provision of lichee nuts."

Mumbling and nattering to himself, the Learned Ming-Tao was escorted from the chamber. The Emperor sadly shook his head. "Ah, Dream-of-Jade, I fear there is no cure for me."

"There is mine," said Dream-of-Jade. "My cure, I promise, will brighten your eyes and quicken your pulse. Your Highness has no appetite? The feast I shall have prepared will be the most delicious you have ever tasted. And tonight, you will sleep more soundly than ever before."

Though doubtful, the Emperor agreed to put himself in the care of Dream-of-Jade, who then departed to issue certain instructions to the cooks and household servants. She soon returned, followed by two attendants bearing between them a heavy log of teakwood.

"Son of Heaven," Dream-of-Jade announced to the puzzled Emperor, "this is the beginning of the feast. Your banquet will arrive shortly. But, in preparation, you will require a pair of chopsticks."

"Imperial Cat," said Kwan-Yu, "already I have a thousand pairs, in gold, silver, ivory, ebony—"

"These will be more valuable than any from your treasure house," Dream-of-Jade answered. "They must be hewn of wood from the center of this log. And, for my cure to be effective, Your Highness himself must cut and shape them."

"What, carve my own chopsticks?" exclaimed Kwan-Yu, as an attendant handed him a small hatchet. "From the center of that log? Impossible!"

Nevertheless, Dream-of-Jade insisted, and grudgingly, Kwan-Yu began chopping away. Soon, blisters covered his hands, sweat drenched his brow, and he begged the cat to let him stop. However, Dream-of-Jade only urged him to greater effort. And soon, indeed, Kwan-Yu's eyes brightened and his pulse quickened from the vigor of his exertions.

At last, when the floor was strewn with chips and nothing remained of the log but two slender pieces of wood, Kwan-Yu threw down the hatchet and mopped his dripping forehead.

Satisfied, Dream-of-Jade nodded. "Is this not as I promised you, Celestial Highness? Already I detect something of a glow about Your Imperial Presence."

Kwan-Yu rubbed his aching arms, then glanced wryly at Dream-of-Jade. "Imperial Cat, you have played a trick on me, though I admit I do feel better than I ever did before. Now, keep the rest of your bargain. All that hacking and chopping has famished me. Never have I been so hungry. Let us enjoy the feast you promised."

At a signal from Dream-of-Jade, the Imperial Cook entered, bearing a huge covered platter that he set before the Emperor. Mouth watering, Kwan-Yu snatched away the cover. His face fell as he stared at the contents, for there was no more than a small bowl of rice.

"Taste it," Dream-of-Jade urged, "and see if it is not more delicious than anything you could ever imagine."

Too hungry to question the humble fare, the ravenous Kwan-Yu seized his newly made chopsticks, plunged them into the bowl, and began gobbling up the rice as if it were a dozen exquisite courses all in one.

"Unbelievably delicious!" exclaimed Kwan-Yu between mouthfuls. "Imperial Cat, this time you have not deceived me. In all my life, I have never tasted anything so marvelous."

Having scooped up every grain of rice, the Emperor yawned sleepily. His muscles ached from unaccustomed labor, and his eyes were so heavy he could scarcely keep them open. Kwan-Yu had never been so eager to go to bed. But when he started toward the Imperial Couch, Dream-of-Jade stepped in front of him and indicated he was to lie, instead, upon a straw mat she had unrolled on the floor.

"What is this?" moaned the Emperor. "I am weary to the marrow of my bones, and you would have me sleep on a mat, without so much as a cushion under my head?"

But Dream-of-Jade insisted, and protesting he would never sleep a wink, Kwan-Yu obeyed. No sooner had he stretched out on the mat than his eyes fell shut, and he plunged into deepest slumber.

Dream-of-Jade watched the Emperor sleeping so soundly, then went to his side and curled up in his arms. Kwan-Yu did not stir until morning. When he woke, his eyes were bright, his appetite keen, and his gloom had altogether vanished.

When Chief Minister Yin-Chuan returned after attending to his urgent state business, he was amazed to find the Emperor in fine health and spirits; but his astonishment soured into dismay when the Emperor shook his finger at him and declared, "This cat has proved herself a better doctor than any of those quacksalvers who would cure me with horoscopes or dose me with unicorn potions and lichee nuts. And as you, Yin-Chuan, look liverish and out of sorts, I command you and all my mandarins to take the same remedy she prescribed for me. Thus you may all enjoy the benefits of her knowledge."

"Do I understand correctly, Celestial Highness," Dream-of-Jade asked, after the crestfallen Chief Minister had bowed his way out of the chamber, "that you judge my treatment a success?"

"You have done all you promised and more," answered Kwan-Yu. "You have taught me a good lesson. But you have also shown me that I am truly fortunate in having a small cat who can be wiser than a great Emperor."

Dream-of-Jade thanked him graciously for such praise. And from then on, whenever she observed the Emperor growing listless or low-spirited, she had only to ask if he wished to repeat her cure. And the mere suggestion was enough to make the Celestial Kwan-Yu recover immediately.

How Dream-of-Jade
Made the Emperor Laugh

"I REQUIRE AMUSEMENT," declared the Emperor. "Honorable Chief Minister Yin-Chuan, you will arrange entertainments to distract me for a little time. I am weary of these dull affairs of state that you so much enjoy and continually force upon me. I have had enough of them today."

"What Your Highness commands is as good as already done even before Your Highness expressed his wishes," replied Yin-Chuan. "I myself shall go to the Department of Lighthearted But Not-Too-Frivolous Diversions. The Master of Tasteful Revelry will devise a program assuring you of every suitably royal delight."

"Get on with it, then," said Kwan-Yu. "The afternoon grows heavier each minute."

The Chief Minister bustled away. Dream-of-Jade, sitting beside the Dragon Throne, pricked up her ears.

"Your Majesty certainly deserves a few carefree moments," she said. "As many as you can find."

"You are right, as usual," said Kwan-Yu. "Imperial Feline, you have no idea how exhausting it is to be a ruler."

"It must be," said Dream-of-Jade, "with an empire so vast."

"No, the empire more or less looks after itself," said Kwan-Yu. "I refer to keeping order among my bickering mandarins and court officials, department heads, assistant department heads—a grievous burden."

"I'm sure His Exceptional Weightiness Yin-Chuan will bring more than enough diversions to make you laugh," said Dream-of-Jade. "Your cares will vanish. Laughter is better than a feast."

"You misunderstand," said Kwan-Yu. "I am Lord of the Middle Kingdom, Rainbow of Celestial Joys—"

"Don't forget Tranquil Carp in the Pool of Crystal Wisdom," put in Dream-of-Jade.

"That, too," said Kwan-Yu. "But I am the Emperor. I do not laugh."

"How can that be?" said Dream-of-Jade. "Even cats laugh—though not in the same way as you human creatures. We laugh with our tails, our whiskers, and often, secretly, within ourselves. If a cat can laugh, so can an emperor."

"Not I." Kwan-Yu shook his head. "I have never gained that mysterious skill."

"What skill?" said Dream-of-Jade. "Take a breath, open your mouth, and do it."

"I am not familiar with that technique," replied Kwan-Yu. "I have studied the martial arts, horsemanship, and archery. The science of laughter is of no use to a monarch. I have, instead, learned each one of the Ninety-five Imperial Attitudes and Gestures.

"I have been carefully taught," Kwan-Yu went on, "to employ the Ferociously Raised Left Eyebrow; the Scowl of Dark Displeasure; the Glance of Withering Devastation, to name but a few. In these, I am most proficient. My Index Finger of Terrifying Menace has been called especially bone-chilling.

"As for laughter, Honorable Yin-Chuan assures me it is inadvisable for an emperor and certainly dangerous. The closest I dare come to it is the Lopsided Smirk."

Dream-of-Jade was distressed to hear this; but, before she could reply, the Chief Minister ushered in a company of acrobats and jugglers. Kwan-Yu folded his arms and silently observed them perform handsprings, cartwheels, and somersaults. They leaped into the air, all the while juggling glittering balls of gold and silver. They balanced chairs on their heads, sprang through flaming hoops, and twirled plates on the tips of bamboo poles.

Dream-of-Jade looked on with a small measure of interest. "They do fairly well," she remarked. "Still, even a kitten could match them in tumbling and gymnastics."

"I have seen these antics many times before," declared Kwan-Yu. "I do not find them amusing. Chief Minister, I hereby raise the Five Fingers of Dismissal."

"Your Highness," Yin-Chuan pleaded, "there is further entertainment in store." He clapped his hands. The acrobats and jugglers withdrew, to be replaced by singers, dancers, an orchestra of flutes, horns, stringed instruments, drums of every shape and size, bronze bells, and half a dozen xylophones.

"Any cat is more lithe and graceful than these dancers," Dream-of-Jade said, barely able to hear herself speak. "In warbling and trilling, a midnight chorus of cats on a rooftop would put these singers to shame. But we would never make such a racket as your Imperial Musicians."

Kwan-Yu put his hands over his ears. "Send them away, Chief Minister. Take yourself away, likewise. And that wretch sawing with his bow—he deserves to be boiled in oil for the sour notes he scratches out."

Crestfallen, the Chief Minister hastily departed along with the singers, dancers, and players. In the empty Throne Room, Kwan-Yu gave the Yawn of Profound Uninterest.

"Tell me, Imperial Feline," he said, "what do cats do when they are bored?"

"That dismal situation does not apply to us," Dream-of-Jade answered. "We cats are never bored. We can, for simplest amusement, always chase our tail. Alas, Your Majesty has no such appendage.

"Or," she added, "we sit quietly and meditate on how fortunate it is to be a cat.

"For a more vigorous activity, we're delighted simply to play with a ball of paper. Would it please you to see a demonstration?"

Kwan-Yu eagerly nodded. "Here," he said, taking a document from the pile at his feet. "This is one of Honorable Yin-Chuan's endless suggestions. Will it do?"

"I can't think of a better purpose," Dream-of-Jade said.

The Emperor tossed the crumpled paper to Dream-of-Jade, who caught it in her forepaws, flung it into the air, rolled over, and caught it again. She batted it back and forth, and scampered after it as if it were trying to escape.

Kwan-Yu brightened a little. "Yes, I find that slightly amusing."

"It would be more so," Dream-of-Jade replied, "if Your Highness did it himself."

"I? Shining Descendant of the Sun and Moon?" exclaimed Kwan-Yu. "Why—why, so I will!"

He sprang from the Dragon Throne, dropped to all fours, and snatched the ball. He rolled over on his back, kicked it with his toes, but it fell far out of his reach.

"For a kitten, less than expert," said Dream-of-Jade. "For an emperor, a good start. But do you find it entertaining? Does it encourage you to laugh?"

"Not entirely," said Kwan-Yu, sitting up and catching his breath. "And yet—yes, there was a moment when I came almost close to a restrained chuckle."

"Still, a good start," said Dream-of-Jade. "We also find great humor playing with a length of string," she added.

"Would Your Majesty care to try? I have something else in mind, as well."

Kwan-Yu unwound the braided cord from around his waist; and, as Dream-of-Jade suggested, he shrugged off his heavy robes of state. In silk shirt and trousers, he waited for Dream-of-Jade's instructions.

"I take one end of the cord in my mouth and run away with it," she said. "You follow and try to catch it. It would be most enjoyable if you chased me on all fours; Your Majesty, however, is not yet ready for that advanced level of amusement."

Trailing the cord, Dream-of-Jade led the Emperor out of the Throne Room. As they sped past the offices of the court officials, the scribes and mandarins dropped their writing brushes and upset their ink pots, dumbstruck to see the Lord of the Middle Kingdom scrambling after a cat and a piece of string. Dream-of-Jade raced on, through hallways and corridors, through the Imperial Kitchens, where the astonished cooks spilled tureens of soup, upset trays of dumplings, and sent baskets of vegetables flying in all directions.

Darting out of a rear door, she passed gardens and groves of willows, heading toward the farthest reaches of the palace grounds. There, she halted. Kwan-Yu wiped his streaming brow.

"Imperial Feline, where have you brought me?" He stared at the crowd of figures dashing back and forth amid the shrubbery, diving and splashing into a pool near a small pavilion, laughing, shouting in merriment.

"We are at the edge of your Forbidden City," Dream-of-Jade replied. "A spot unvisited by your courtiers, overlooked, and forgotten."

"And who are those diminutive creatures?" Kwan-Yu demanded.

"They are a few of your subjects," Dream-of-Jade answered. "The smallest, surely the humblest, who come here secretly to play. They are children."

"Children?" said Kwan-Yu. "Ah, yes. I have heard of such beings. I never realized they were so short."

"Your Highness," Dream-of-Jade said, "how can you not recognize children? You yourself were once a child."

"Never," said Kwan-Yu. "I was born Celestial Emperor."

"Every cat was born a kitten," said Dream-of-Jade. "The same principle applies to a Celestial Emperor."

"I do not remember being in such a condition," replied Kwan-Yu. "But if you, my trusted companion, say it is so, I must believe you. Why, though, do they come here in secret?"

"Like all your subjects, they are forbidden to set foot even in a forgotten corner of your palace grounds," answered Dream-of-Jade. "However, since no one comes here, they know they will not be discovered."

"They seem highly amused by their occupations," said Kwan-Yu. "Is it possible for us to join them?"

"That would be a good start," said Dream-of-Jade.

The children, overjoyed to see Dream-of-Jade, welcomed her as a familiar friend. Not recognizing Emperor Kwan-Yu, they allowed him to play their games, leapfrogged over his back, dodged nimbly when he tried to tag them, and always found him in hide-and-seek.

Soon, Kwan-Yu felt his sides shaking and unusual noises bursting from his lips.

"Imperial Feline," he cried, "what is happening to me?"

"I would guess," answered Dream-of-Jade, "Your Majesty is laughing."

"Remarkable!" exclaimed Kwan-Yu. "I wish to do more of it."

That instant, the children suddenly raced away and vanished. For now arrived all the mandarins, cooks, a company of guards; and, at their head, the Chief Minister himself.

"Your Majesty, have you been harmed?" demanded Yin-Chuan, hurrying toward him. "I have been told you were seen rolling on the ground, running through the palace. And now this!"

"I am undamaged," said Kwan-Yu. "I have been playing with—what do you call them, Imperial Feline? Children."

"Have no fear," said Yin-Chuan, shocked. "I will make certain it does not happen again."

"No, you will not," retorted Kwan-Yu. "I wish it to happen again, and as often as I please."

"Allow me to suggest," put in Dream-of-Jade, "it would be more fitting if the children did not have to come secretly. Turn these grounds into an open park and let all your subjects freely visit. Not only for the sake of the children but, as well, for the sake of the child you once were—and the child still living in the back of your memory."

"So it will be done," declared Kwan-Yu. "Let it be called the Garden of the Emperor's Laughter."

"Your Highness," the Chief Minister sputtered, "this cat has driven you mad."

"On the contrary, she has driven me sane," said Kwan-Yu. "She has helped me to laugh and made me a little wiser today than I was yesterday."

"A good start," said Dream-of-Jade.

How Dream-of-Jade Chose a Gift

THE EMPEROR KWAN-YU woke up one morning to find himself filled with a most unusual sensation. It so puzzled him that he asked his beloved white cat, Dream-of-Jade, what such a feeling might be.

"Can Your Celestial Highness describe it?" said Dream-of-Jade, who had been curled at the foot of the Imperial Couch of Blissful Repose. "Would you call it pleasant? Or unpleasant? Cold and rough? Or warm and fuzzy?"

"Altogether pleasant," said Kwan-Yu. "Warm, yes; and, indeed rather fuzzy around the edges. It gives me an overpowering urge to do a kindness of some sort, in exchange for kindness that a certain individual has done for me. Can you, Imperial Feline, identify this condition?"

"In my considered opinion," Dream-of-Jade replied, "Your Highness has come down with a simple case of: gratitude."

"Good heavens!" cried the Emperor. "Is it serious?"

"Serious but never fatal. Your Highness will surely recover from it," Dream-of-Jade replied. "The customary remedy is to offer a gift in token of appreciation."

"Then," declared Kwan-Yu, "I will do so immediately."

Without waiting for his Breakfast of Seventy-four Delicious Aromas and Flavors, still in his night robe, and Dream-of-Jade padding along beside him, Kwan-Yu hurried to the Hall of Joyful Morning Proclamations.

There, his waiting courtiers and palace officials bowed their heads to the ground. While Kwan-Yu seated himself on his throne, Chief Minister Yin-Chuan waddled up with an armload of scrolls.

"I fervently hope Your Highness has experienced delightful slumbers and happiest dreams," the Chief Minister began. "I trust Your Glorious Majesty is sufficiently refreshed to turn his Eagle Eye of Keen Attention to questions demanding his wise decisions."

"If you're talking about the usual affairs of state," put in Dream-of-Jade, "such as which mandarin will be allowed to wear a button on his cap and who gets promoted from third to second rank, and if you mean to drone on about them all morning, you'll bore His Majesty back to sleep."

"Please, please, Imperial Feline," Kwan-Yu gently chided, "Yin-Chuan is an official of the highest position. Do try to show him a little respect."

"I will," said Dream-of-Jade. "As little as possible."

"Honorable Yin-Chuan," continued the Emperor, "all other business must be put aside. I have been informed by reliable diagnosis that I am afflicted with gratitude."

The courtiers flung up their hands and gasped in horror. The Chief Minister's eyes popped open as wide as his gaping mouth. At last, after some speechless moments, he said:

"Is Your Highness absolutely certain? Perhaps it is only a passing indigestion. If Your Highness immersed his Celestial Head in a cooling bath, the condition might go away."

"I do not wish to immerse my head," Kwan-Yu said. "I wish to take prompt action."

"As Chief Minister, it is my duty to express deepest disapproval," Yin-Chuan said. "Gratitude? In an emperor? Unheard of! In all the history of the Middle Kingdom there has never been an example of it. Indeed, the less gratitude the better. It could, heaven forbid, lead to generosity. It might"—Yin-Chuan's voice dropped to a fearful whisper—"it might even be contagious."

"Don't worry. I'm sure you're immune," said Dream-of-Jade. "But, yes, what a confusing state of affairs if everyone went around being grateful and generous."

"For once, Imperial Feline," said Yin-Chuan, "you demonstrate a flicker of intelligence."

"And yet," Dream-of-Jade went on, "I believe gratitude is one of the Nine Heavenly Virtues."

"Ah—possibly," Yin-Chuan admitted. "They have slipped my mind, they are so seldom invoked. I would have to consult the Department of Honorable Conduct."

"And is it not true," added Dream-of-Jade, "His Majesty is called the Embodiment of Nine Heavenly Virtues?"

"He may embody them," retorted Yin-Chuan. "That does not mean he is expected to practice them."

"I will hear no further discussion," said Kwan-Yu. "My mind is made up. I will, this very day, bestow a gift upon my wise councilor, my trusted adviser—"

"Indeed?" A syrupy smile trickled over Yin-Chuan's face. "Ah, yes, that would be an entirely different matter. If Your Majesty wishes to reward the one who stands closest to you, whose every thought is directed toward your benefit and well-being—yes, quite correct and admirable. Such a gift, of course, must be handsome, grand; in short, worthy of the giver."

Yin-Chuan lowered his voice and whispered in the Emperor's ear. "Your Highness displays his usual grace and delicacy. Let me say, between ourselves, I perfectly understand. Your Highness refers to his humble, modest, eminently deserving servant: none other than myself."

"I refer," said Kwan-Yu, "to the Imperial Feline, my dear and trusted Dream-of-Jade."

Yin-Chuan's smile dribbled away. "A royal gift to a common cat?" he exclaimed. "Your Majesty cannot be serious. No, no, I see now Your Highness is jesting. A delightful joke. Observe, Your Majesty, that I applaud your sublime humor."

The courtiers, following the Chief Minister's example, all clapped their hands. Kwan-Yu frowned.

"Silence! You have heard what I have spoken. The only question: What shall be the gift? Chief Minister,

I ask for your most thoughtful and carefully considered recommendations."

"Your Majesty," replied Yin-Chuan, choking as if a prickly pear had stuck in his gullet, "I have one fitting suggestion. First, I must point out that the recipient of your inestimable largesse is nothing but a cat."

"You tell me what I already know," snapped Kwan-Yu.

"Therefore," Yin-Chuan went on, "she has no need of money, precious gems, embroidered garments. And so I advise an ample, adequate, and appropriate reward."

"Which is?"

"I suggest," said Yin-Chuan, "from the Imperial Kitchens, a few discarded fish heads."

"Would you disgrace me?" Kwan-Yu retorted. "By your own words, the gift must be worthy of the giver." He turned to Dream-of-Jade. "You, my Honored Feline, shall choose whatever pleases you."

"If Your Majesty so wishes," Dream-of-Jade replied, calmly grooming her whiskers, "I shall be happy to oblige."

The Chief Minister ground his teeth and muttered to himself as Kwan-Yu commanded the palace attendants to fetch treasures from the Glittering Repository of Highly Valuable Objects.

Dream-of-Jade kept grooming her whiskers. The attendants soon returned with trays, baskets, coffers, chests, bins, and barrels. At a gesture from Kwan-Yu, they unloaded the objects and spread them in a dazzling display.

"If you see nothing that captures your interest," said Kwan-Yu, "I shall have more treasures brought for your consideration."

Dream-of-Jade kept grooming her whiskers.

"First, however," said Kwan-Yu, waving a hand at the array, "let me point out an item or two that you may find attractive. Here, for your restful repose, these cushions filled with softest down from the Imperial Swans, and embroidered with threads of pure gold and silver."

Dream-of-Jade kept grooming her whiskers. "Most luxurious," she said, "but I'm perfectly happy with my present sleeping accommodations on your couch."

"Then," said Kwan-Yu, "perhaps this pair of porcelain vases, thin as eggshells? This figurine carved from a piece of flawless crystal? Or, in the way of personal adornment, these necklaces of perfectly matched pearls? These rings and bracelets, this brooch of amethyst, rubies, and emeralds?"

Dream-of-Jade kept grooming her whiskers. "Each one a treasure, no doubt," she said, "but of no practical use to me."

"It is as I told you, Imperial Highness," the Chief Minister burst out. "This cat has no appreciation of the finer things in life. Throw her a fish head and be done with it. Talk of gratitude? This creature turns up her nose at all she sees. She means to make fools of us."

"Extremely Honorable Chief Minister," put in Dream-of-Jade, "no one can make a fool of you unless you are a fool to begin with."

"I realize, Imperial Feline," said Kwan-Yu, "my possessions hold no interest for you. Added all together, they come to far less than you deserve.

"Name whatever else you desire," he added. "I give you my solemn promise: Your wish will be granted."

Dream-of-Jade stopped grooming her whiskers. "Is that indeed so?"

"You have my word," Kwan-Yu replied.

"In that case," said Dream-of-Jade, without a moment's hesitation, "I ask a portion of Your Majesty's kingdom."

"What? What? What?" Chief Minister Yin-Chuan went off like a string of firecrackers. He rolled up his eyes and clutched his head. "Imperial Highness, this cat goes too far! How dare she make such a request? A portion of your kingdom? No, no! Impossible!"

Kwan-Yu was silent. At last, he slowly nodded.

"So I have promised," he said in a quiet voice. "So it will be."

"Folly! Madness!" roared the Chief Minister. "What monarch ever keeps a promise?"

"And yet," said Dream-of-Jade, "I believe that keeping one's word is another of the Nine Heavenly Virtues."

"Heavenly tripe!" The Chief Minister shook a fist at Dream-of-Jade. "Speak no more of them. Nine virtues? Nine too many!"

"Bring maps of my realm," ordered Kwan-Yu. "The Imperial Feline shall choose her portion."

"What if she wants a whole province? Or more?" blurted the Chief Minister. "Perhaps she could be persuaded to accept a few acres of weeds? A parcel of out-of-the-way real estate?"

"Do as I command," said Kwan-Yu. "Go seek charts and surveys of every town and village, mountain, lake, and river."

"They will not be necessary," Dream-of-Jade said, as Yin-Chuan stormed off.

"But, Imperial Feline," said Kwan-Yu, "how else shall you know what to choose?"

"First," said Dream-of-Jade, "I merely wished to see if Your Majesty would, in fact, keep his word. Which you have done most admirably."

"And the portion of my kingdom?" Kwan-Yu frowned, perplexed and puzzled. "What of that?"

"The Middle Kingdom is vast," answered Dream-of-Jade. "But there is another kingdom even greater: the kingdom within Your Majesty's heart.

"It is of that kingdom," Dream-of-Jade continued, "I wish a small corner."

"My dear companion, you have that already." Kwan-Yu knelt to stroke Dream-of-Jade. "It is no small corner, but the largest and happiest. What of your gift?"

"My wish," said Dream-of-Jade, "is for Your Majesty to become the best of all rulers. I admit," she added, "that may take a little while."

"Again, you have my word," Kwan-Yu said fondly. "I shall make every effort."

"I ask no more than that," said Dream-of-Jade.

"Perhaps the Nine Heavenly Virtues may be of some use," said Kwan-Yu. "I will have my Chief Scribe write each one down so I can keep the list before me at all times."

"No need," said Dream-of-Jade. "I'd be glad to point them out to you, but Your Highness will surely discover them for yourself along the way."

And Dream-of-Jade went back to grooming her whiskers.

How Dream-of-Jade
Wrote the Law

THE CELESTIAL EMPEROR Kwan-Yu was determined to rule his kingdom well, so he commanded his Chief Minister Yin-Chuan and his mandarins to prepare new tables of laws. When, at last, the scrolls were brought for the Emperor to read and approve, Kwan-Yu summoned his beloved white cat, Dream-of-Jade, to sit beside him in the Chamber of Enlightened Edicts.

"This will be of great benefit and illumination for you," the Emperor told her. "There have been moments, Imperial Cat, when you have not accorded my ministers and mandarins all the honor and respect that is their due. But I have no doubt your opinion will change once you have read these new proclamations."

"Son of Heaven," Dream-of-Jade answered, "I only wish I were as confident."

"You will see for yourself," said the Emperor. "Scholars and statesmen have labored day and night, studying, debating, and pondering every detail. The keenest intellects have examined and refined each regulation. Nothing has been overlooked."

The Chief Minister Yin-Chuan, who was attending the Emperor, sagely nodded his head. "That is true, Celestial Highness. However, allow your unworthy servant to add one humble rectification. These laws have been drafted under my constant supervision. I am proud to take full responsibility for them. As it is written in the Maxims of the First Emperor: The hand may govern the fingers, but the head governs the hand. While you, Tranquil Carp, are the radiant head, I believe I may say in all modesty that none of these endeavors would have been accomplished without my guiding hand."

"Your brilliance is truly unbelievable," Dream-of-Jade said, turning her beautiful green eyes on Yin-Chuan with such an admiring gaze that the Chief Minister could not conceal a self-satisfied smile. "Surely, Honorable Yin-Chuan, no one in all the Middle Kingdom has a mind like yours."

At each word from Dream-of-Jade, Yin-Chuan puffed himself up a little more. He beamed and smirked as she continued. "How difficult your task must have been. How demanding of all your powers. What effort surely was required."

"Highness," Yin-Chuan said, "indeed, this cat shows unexpected perspicacity."

"And yet," said Dream-of-Jade, "and yet, Honorable Yin-Chuan, it occurs to me that your task was not, after all, in the least way difficult."

The Chief Minister bristled, and his smile melted away. "Not difficult? Unlettered cat! How dare you say this?"

"It seems to me," Dream-of-Jade calmly replied, "to one of brilliant intellect, nothing can be all that difficult. What may appear impossibly hard to one of little talent is a mere trifle to one of unquestionable genius. Therefore, Honorable Yin-Chuan, the greater one's ability, the less credit is deserved. Do we praise the elephant for bearing a heavy burden so easily? Whereas, if an ant were to do the same, it would be more worthy of admiration. Is that not the case, Yin-Chuan?"

The Chief Minister squirmed uncomfortably. Dream-of-Jade went on, "You spoke of a guiding hand, Honorable Yin-Chuan. And yet, which threads a needle, the fingers or the palm? Consider not only your own remarkable endowments, but the assistance of your clerks and scholars as well.

"Indeed, as I think of it," Dream-of-Jade added, "this enterprise must have been altogether simple for you. Even a cat could have done as well."

"A cat?" burst out Yin-Chuan. "An ignorant beast do as well as a Chief Minister? Arrogant feline! Next, will you claim you can rule better than the Emperor himself?"

Kwan-Yu had been following Dream-of-Jade's argument with interest, but now he laughed gently and stroked the cat's silken white fur.

"My dearest companion," Kwan-Yu said to her, "you are a most beautiful creature and, undeniably, a helpful one. This time, however, I fear you have overstepped yourself. The making of laws is the affair of humans, not animals, and a burden even for the wisest. Be grateful it is a burden you need not bear."

But Yin-Chuan still smarted from Dream-of-Jade's reproach, and he furiously broke in, "No, no, Celestial Highness! Let her see for herself whether it is easy. I challenge her to surpass my accomplishment, to prepare even a single decree!"

"An interesting suggestion," replied Kwan-Yu, with a thoughtful smile. "She has always been quick to teach me lessons, now she may learn one in her turn. Nevertheless, it must be done in all fairness. A cat cannot be expected to understand the nature of human justice. Therefore, her law must deal with matters pertaining to her own species. Imperial Cat, do you agree to this?"

"Willingly," answered Dream-of-Jade. "I shall proclaim my law here and now, and you shall judge its merit for yourself."

The Emperor nodded. But the Chief Minister gave Dream-of-Jade a scornful glance. "Honorable Mandarin, Chief Minister of Cats," he said mockingly, "High Magistrate of Feline Affairs, favor us with your decree."

Dream-of-Jade drew herself up, draped her tail over her paws as if donning a judge's gown, and solemnly began. "Whereas, it is hereby decreed to all felines of the Middle Kingdom: They are enjoined to observe every provision of the judicial codes unless such provisions aforesaid have been abrogated heretofore, though any abrogation is liable to reinstatement at any time whatever and shall be effective retroactively without recourse on behalf of said felines whether or not said felines are presently or will be engaged in litigation. This decree is not susceptible to appeal."

"Imperial Cat!" cried the Emperor, holding his head. "What kind of law is this? Though I never expected the wisdom of a Court Councilor from you, this decree you propose is utter nonsense!"

"So it is, Imperial Highness," Yin-Chuan triumphantly declared. "Incomprehensible! Ridiculous! As I knew it would be. This proves my point exactly." He turned, gloating, to Dream-of-Jade. "Ignorant, pretentious animal! What have you now to say for yourself?"

Dream-of-Jade humbly bowed her head. "Honorable Yin-Chuan, I agree with the Emperor's opinion."

"There, Son of Heaven," cried Yin-Chuan, "you hear it from this cat's own mouth! She confesses her incompetence and stupidity!"

"That is not precisely what I said, Worthy Councilor," Dream-of-Jade returned. "True, your reproach is well founded. However, allow me to explain—"

Yin-Chuan snorted. "No explanation is needed. Such nonsense is absolutely inexcusable."

"Nevertheless," Dream-of-Jade replied, "I must point out that my decree does no more than repeat what you yourself have written. I merely employed the word 'feline' where your proclamation stated 'subjects of the Emperor.' Honorable Yin-Chuan, the decree is not mine, but yours."

Yin-Chuan's face swelled with rage, but before he could sputter a protest, Dream-of-Jade sprang to the Emperor's table, spread out the scrolls, and with a paw indicated the decree written by the Chief Minster's own hand.

"It is as you say, Imperial Cat," murmured the Emperor, frowning. "But how could you have known this?"

"I have already studied the scrolls," Dream-of-Jade answered. "Each night, when the Honorable Yin-Chuan and his mandarins finished their work, I went to the Judicial Chambers and examined what they had done.

"As they are so confident of their ability, they never trouble to read what they have written, and so, alas, they forget what they have inscribed from one day to the next. It is true; Yin-Chuan is highly capable. Capable, that is, of proclaiming one thing today and the opposite tomorrow."

"Do you mean to tell me that all these proclamations are as ridiculous as the first?" cried the Emperor.

"No, Celestial Highness," said Dream-of-Jade. "They are even more so. In comparison, what I pronounced was a model of clarity."

Hearing this, Kwan-Yu snatched up the scrolls and flung them at the head of the cowering Chief Minister. "My cat will write laws for me, and they will be far better than yours," he shouted. "Yin-Chuan, as of this moment you are reduced to the rank of Clerk-Scribe of the Twenty-fifth Order. Be gone! Out of my sight!"

Robes flapping, sandals flying, Yin-Chuan retreated from the chamber as fast as his bulk allowed, terrified that worse might befall him.

Dream-of-Jade, however, shook her head and glanced anxiously at the Emperor. "Lord of the Middle Kingdom," she said, "I shall be happy to draw up whatever laws may be required. But I fear you have acted hastily. For now you have deprived yourself of the services of a Chief Minister."

"No, Imperial Cat," answered Kwan-Yu. "My Chief Minister is here at my right hand, as she should be."

"This is a great honor," Dream-of-Jade modestly replied. "But surely Your Highness is aware that never in the history of the Middle Kingdom has an emperor had a cat for a councilor."

"Then it is high time," said the Emperor. "And, in any case, never before has there been a cat like you."

"If Your Celestial Highness says so," replied Dream-of-Jade, smiling, "would anyone dare to disagree?"

And so, Dream-of-Jade wrote the Emperor's new code of laws, and from that day forward, no edict was proclaimed nor matter of state decided without the advice and approval of the Emperor's Chief Minister, his beloved Dream-of-Jade. All prospered in the Middle Kingdom, and in the Archives of the Emperors, the reign of Celestial Kwan-Yu was inscribed in letters of gold as the happiest and wisest.